*Plea Of The Damned 6
Forgive Me Dawson*

Plea Of The Damned 6 Forgive Me Dawson

Avril Sabine

Cracked Acorn Productions
Australia

Plea Of The Damned 6: Forgive Me Dawson

Published by

Cracked Acorn Productions

PO Box 1365

Gympie, Queensland 4570

Australia

978-1-925941-04-3 (Kindle)

978-1-925941-05-0 (EPUB)

978-1-925941-06-7 (Print)

Genre: Young Adult Urban Fantasy/Paranormal

Cover design by Caitlyn Petersen

Dedication

For those who choose to make a difference,
even if it is the harder path to travel.

Plea Of The Damned

Have you ever done something and immediately wished you could undo it? Jack knows that feeling very well. He's damned, bound to haunt his old school and help students until he atones for his sins. It's the last thing he wants to do. But since the alternative is an eternity in hell, he's not about to say no.

Book 6: Forgive Me Dawson

After years of being forced to live with his aunt and uncle, Dawson is finally allowed to move in with his brother. If he can stay out of trouble, he'll get to stay. When old troubles surface, he begins to worry they'll ruin more than his chances to remain with his brother. They might risk his life.

*

This story was written by an Australian author using Australian spelling.

Chapter One

Jack

Jack stood out the front of the groundsman's shed, wishing he had a watch. Or some other way to tell the time. Marti had visited him every Saturday afternoon all throughout term. Without fail. Each time she'd told him she'd be back the next Saturday, at half past four. She'd said the same thing last week, but this was the first Saturday of her school holidays. School had ended for the year for her grade. Year ten had finished at the same time as year eleven and the year twelves had finished the previous week. Only years seven, eight and nine hadn't finished. They didn't go on holidays until early December.

He scanned the area, certain it had to be after half past four. She was never late. What if something had happened to her? No, surely it was just a case of her having forgotten it was the start of her school holidays when she'd spoken to him. Or the phrase had become automatic. Last Saturday she'd been excited about contacting another one of the kids he'd helped. They'd been in touch with her through the website she'd created. A smile fleetingly appeared and he slowly shook his head. He couldn't believe she'd created the Jack Richards Fan Club. And had now managed to contact all those he'd helped. She hadn't met up with any of them yet. Hadn't had time since the website had only been active for a couple of weeks and she'd been busy with exams and the end of the school year. As had the rest of them.

Again he scanned the area. Nothing moved. The afternoon was still, the school grounds deserted. She had to be all right. A hand curled into a fist and he wanted to strike out at something at the frustration that arrowed through him. There wasn't anyone he could ask. Not even that blasted bird was likely to tell him if something had happened to Marti. It had been hard not being able to talk to her when she visited. There were things he'd wanted to tell her. Such as when one of the others was likely to visit. They all visited him, at various times, just none as frequently or as regularly as Marti. She really wanted to meet one of them, but was worried about someone falsely claiming they knew him so they could set up a meeting with her.

"Here I was thinking you were actually beginning to improve and instead I find you looking like you want to start a fight."

Jack turned towards the angel, somehow managing not to sigh heavily. Typical of his luck. Why couldn't that blasted bird have turned up this morning? Or even a couple of hours earlier. "Marti isn't here. She said she'd be here this afternoon."

"She's no longer your concern. None of them are. There is another in need of your help."

Somehow he managed not to let his hands curl into fists again. It was close. The blasted bird always brought out the worst in him. He'd known he would receive no answers and yet he hadn't been able to stop himself from saying what he was worried about. "What is the kid's name?"

The angel met his gaze. "Don't change the subject. Do you understand? Marti, and the others you've helped, are no longer your concern."

"What if they want to visit me?"

"That is up to them. Their choice. They are welcome to exercise their free will. What isn't acceptable is you demanding answers as to their whereabouts or what they're doing with their lives now."

Jack remained silent even though he wanted to disagree. What could it hurt for the blasted bird to answer a few questions?

"Do you understand?"

"I heard you." He wasn't about to say he understood when he certainly didn't. Unless it was yet one more punishment. That wouldn't surprise him at all.

The angel studied him. "Yet I don't think it has made a difference. You might have heard, but I feel you haven't listened."

"I heard and listened." Again he had to force himself to keep his hands still when he was tempted to curl them into fists. It didn't matter what he did, the blasted bird always thought the worst of him.

Again the angel studied him. "His name is Dawson."

"And I guess you can't tell me anything else about him." He'd probably let more sarcasm enter his tone than he should have, but the blasted bird knew exactly how to annoy him.

The angel smiled. "The two of you actually have a lot in common."

He almost asked what it was they had in common,

but doubted he'd receive an answer. The blasted bird had probably only given him the extra information because he'd said he wouldn't give out any details. All he could hope was that Dawson didn't have his tendency to screw things up.

"I'm sure you'll have a lot to talk about." With another smile, the angel vanished.

Jack took a step forward, tempted to call out to the angel. He'd been told even less than usual. How was he meant to recognise the kid he was meant to help? And when would he turn up? It had probably been deliberate. No wonder half the time he didn't think the angel wanted the kids to have a chance.

Being told a name and that they had a lot in common wasn't in the least bit useful. And having something in common didn't sound good at all. There were a lot of things about himself he wouldn't wish on anyone. Such as completely screwing up his life when his mother died and accidentally shooting Rose.

He tried to think of which student might be Dawson. There were three of them at the school. One of them in year seven and the other two in year eleven. The youngest one was shy and he didn't know much about him. Of the other two, one was heavily into sports with a solid build and the other one kept to himself, was tall and slim and frequently carried a sketchpad around.

He scanned the area. There was no one. Not Marti and not Dawson. That blasted bird could have told him what had happened to Marti. She wouldn't return to school for months. He couldn't wait that long to find out what had happened to her. Or worse. Never find out at all. What if he asked Dawson to contact her through the website? Surely it couldn't hurt to do that. And even if it annoyed the blasted bird, what else could he do to him?

Jack sighed. He'd probably find some way to cause problems. What if they sent him to hell instead of giving him the chance to atone for his sins? Who'd help the students then? He remained where he was, trying to decide what to do, all the time hoping Marti would turn up so he could stop worrying about her.

Chapter Two

Dawson

Hearing a notification on his phone, Dawson glared at it as he set his pencil down on the sketchpad he had open on the kitchen table. He wasn't expecting anyone to contact him. He ran his fingers through his sandy brown hair, pushing it out of his eyes. His brother kept telling him he needed a haircut, but there were always other things to do. His green eyes were drawn to the sketchpad. More interesting things to do. He picked up his pencil. Whoever it was, they could wait. He didn't get the chance to continue before another message came through. They were persistent. Setting his pencil down, he picked up his phone that was also on the kitchen table. The messages were from Levi, the last person in the world he'd ever expected to contact him again.

Need to meet up. Problem with the item you gave me.

Dawson frowned. Item? The only thing he'd ever given Levi was a forged permission slip and that was months ago. He hadn't had anything to do with him before or since and planned to keep it that way.

Can't. Have plans.

Break them. This is important.

There was no way he'd break these plans. His brother was taking him out to dinner tonight, when he got home from work, to celebrate the end of the school year. Just like their parents used to do on the first Saturday night after the end of school. Back when they were alive. He'd shrugged when Morgan had suggested it, but was actually looking forward to going. This was the first year he'd been able to live with his brother. He'd been stuck living with his aunt and uncle before that. And there was no way he wanted to endure that again. He was sixteen. It wasn't like he was some little kid. There shouldn't have been so many dramas about moving in with Morgan. His phone signalled another text.

Meet me at school. Now. I had to say who gave me the item.

He glared at the phone. This was why he didn't forge permission slips for anyone other than close friends. Not that he had many of them these days.

Most of them had dropped out of his life during the first few months after his parents had died. Although he couldn't blame them. If Levi hadn't caught him forging one during lunch, a few months back, he never would have agreed. He sighed heavily when another message came through.

Someone found it and threatened to go to the cops. I think we can talk them out of it if you meet up with me at school. Not like anyone else should be there. Most of the grades are on holidays now and who hangs around school when they're on school holidays?

He would kill Levi. Pushing the chair back from the table, he glanced wistfully at the sketch of Cerberus fighting a demon before replying. *When?*

Now.

Be there in fifteen.

Okay.

Leaving the drawing on the table, he slipped his phone into a pocket of his jeans before grabbing his sneakers and heading for the front door. Just when he'd finally figured out how to draw the demon's expression. He hated being interrupted while a drawing was going well. Anger rushed through him as he thought of all the drawings his uncle had torn up during the few years he'd lived with them. Yelling at him that he was wasting his time like his father once had. And that his life would go nowhere if he didn't figure out what he wanted to do with it and focus on his schoolwork instead of his drawings.

Taking a deep breath, he tried to let the anger go. It was hard. Almost impossible. He'd promised Morgan he wouldn't get in any more fights. So far he'd lasted five weeks and two days. It looked like this afternoon was really going to test his ability to keep his promise. Not to mention some of the other promises he'd made. Like staying out of trouble.

It didn't take long to reach the school grounds and instead of walking around to the main entrance, he vaulted over the fence. A glance around showed him the place was empty. Taking out his phone, he sent Levi a message, asking him where he was.

Where are you?

He kept walking as he sent a reply to Levi. *Not far from the groundsman's shed.*

Meet you there.

Dawson made his way to the front of the groundsman's shed, stopping several metres from the front door when he saw someone stood out the front. He was about to message Levi and let him know someone was already there, when he came into sight, a man walking beside him. They both had dark hair and broad shoulders, their expressions and features similar enough that he assumed they were related.

Levi stopped within arm's reach of Dawson, nodding towards the man with him. "My dad. Burke."

Burke gave him a nod in greeting, one hand tucked into a pocket of his faded jeans. "Saw the permission slip you did for Levi."

Dawson glanced at the young man who stood in front of the groundsman's shed, neither of them paying him any attention. He guessed he must be with them. Not that he looked anything like someone they'd associate with. Even though they all wore jeans and t-shirts, Levi and his father had bands on their shirts while the one who stood in front of the shed had a plain white t-shirt with a leather jacket over it and a hairstyle that made him seem like he'd stepped out of the early nineteen sixties. Levi and his father looked like they avoided hairdressers and barbers and hacked their hair off with blunt scissors. He studied the way their hair fell around their faces, imagining how he could recreate it in a drawing.

"Are you listening to me, Dawson?" Burke demanded.

Dawson nodded, glancing at the guy in the leather jacket who had come closer. "What did you want me to say? Sorry?" That was what his uncle always wanted him to say. Even when it wasn't his fault. Although according to his uncle, he was always to blame.

"How long did it take you to copy my handwriting and signature?" Burke asked.

"What?" Surely he hadn't heard him correctly. What did that have to do with anything?

"Didn't you just finish telling me you were listening?" Burke asked.

Chapter Three

Dawson

Dawson's first instinct was to give a sarcastic reply. He barely held the words back, reminding himself once again of the many promises he'd made to his brother. They basically could be summed up with a single promise. That of staying out of trouble.

"Well?" Burke took a step closer, taking his hand out of his pocket. "Don't ignore me."

"I don't know what you want." Dawson glanced at the guy in the leather jacket who'd also come closer.

"Answer the question. How long did it take to write the permission slip and what did you use to do it so accurately?" Burke demanded. "And how did you learn to do it so well?"

"A letter. Or something with enough writing on it to get an idea of how you form your letters and numbers and something with your signature on it." Dawson sent a look in Levi's direction, that promised payback. "It's how I learned to draw. Copying everything. From images to writing. Studying how other people did things."

"How long?"

The entire conversation made little sense. Dawson shrugged. Did Burke want to know how long he'd been drawing or how long he'd taken to forge his handwriting.

"Answer me," Burke snapped. "How long did it take you to do the permission slip?"

Dawson was tempted to tell him he should have stated the question that clearly to start with. "An hour or so. Your handwriting isn't that complicated."

"How about cursive writing?" Burke asked.

Dawson frowned. "I don't get what you mean." Why wasn't he talking about ethics and wanting to discuss this with his parents? That's what normally happened in these types of situations. And he should know after all the times he'd been in trouble. Something wasn't right. He glanced at the guy in the leather jacket who watched everything that was happening. Why did he just stand there saying nothing and why hadn't Levi introduced him too?

"Not very bright, are you?" Burke said.

Dawson tried to ignore Levi's grin, but it was hard. He let his breath out slowly, focusing on letting go of his anger along with it. Not that it helped. "Maybe you better spell it out nice and clear then." He couldn't keep the dry tone from his voice.

Burke closed the distance between them, a good half a head taller than Dawson. He looked down at him, his broad shoulders blocking out most of the remaining light of the day. "Don't take that tone with me, boy."

Dawson's hands curled into fists and it took all of his willpower not to take a swing at Burke. "I need to get home or my brother will come looking for me."

"You told him where you were going?" Burke remained menacingly close.

Dawson refused to step back even though he really wanted to. He noticed the guy in the leather jacket was almost as close as Burke. What was he doing here and should he demand an introduction? "He expects me to leave him a message to let him know where I'm going." It was a pity he hadn't done as he was meant to. No one knew where he was or who he was meeting.

"You're going to get yourself killed standing up to him like that, Dawson."

He looked at the guy in the leather jacket when he spoke, about to speak to him when he spoke again.

"I'm Jack Richards, by the way. A ghost. So you might not want to talk to me unless you want them to think you're crazy." He waved his hand in front of Burke's face before waving it through his head several times.

Dawson took a step back, unable to take his gaze off Jack. He closed his mouth when he realised it was open. What was going on? Was this some kind of prank? He glanced between Levi and Jack.

Burke looked in Jack's direction. "What do you keep looking at? Is this some kind of setup?" He grabbed Dawson by the shoulder. "That's it. We're finding somewhere else to talk."

Dawson tried to pull away from Burke, but the man's grip tightened on his shoulder.

Jack walked beside him. "Play along for now. See what he wants. Then make a run for it the first chance you get."

Dawson looked at each of them. Burke who gripped his shoulder, Levi who grinned every time he looked at him and Jack who kept scanning the area like he was expecting something to happen. "Look, I don't-"

"Keep your mouth shut." Burke kept walking, forcing Dawson to keep pace with his lengthy stride.

Dawson started to speak again, getting as far as opening his mouth before Jack spoke.

"I'd do as he says if I was you. The sooner he tells you what he wants, the sooner he might get out of here." Jack scanned the area again. "I should have told her not to visit when I had the chance."

Dawson wasn't sure if he should ask Jack who he was talking about. Nothing made sense. Not the way Burke was behaving and not the fact Jack didn't seem solid.

Arriving near one of the classrooms, Burke came to a stop, facing Dawson. "I don't have all day. Can you do cursive writing?"

"I can copy anything with a bit of practice." Dawson glanced at Jack. Maybe he'd taken that swing at Burke earlier and he'd been knocked out. This was all in his mind and he was actually passed out on the ground in front of the groundsman's shed. Lucky it was nearly summer and they weren't in for a cold night.

Burke let go of his shoulder and took out a folded piece of paper from a pocket of his jeans. It was creased and he flattened it out before he unfolded it. "Can you do this?"

He frowned, his gaze drawn to each of the images that had been photocopied. "Cheque stubs? No one uses cheques these days."

"Old people do," Levi said.

Burke backhanded Levi. "I told you to keep your mouth shut."

Levi glared at the ground. "Like he won't be able to figure it out." He took a step back when his father started to raise his hand again. "He's not that much of an idiot." He glanced up, taking another step away from his father, remaining quiet this time.

Burke stared at his son a moment longer before he faced Dawson. "I'll expect you back here tomorrow afternoon with all that copied out." He drew out another piece of paper, holding both of them out to Dawson. "And here's the signature."

Chapter Four

Dawson

Dawson didn't take the pieces of paper from Burke. There was no way he was going to get involved. His brother would kill him. And he'd probably end up back with his aunt and uncle. Which would be worse than his brother wanting to kill him.

Burke shook the paper. "What are you waiting for?"

"I don't think it's a request," Jack said. "You better take the paper before you're the one he's backhanding."

Dawson took the two pieces of paper from Burke, not bothering to unfold the second one. "What if I can't copy it that quickly?"

"You better hope you can." Burke stepped close to

him again, grabbing a fistful of his shirt. "And you better not say anything to anyone or you'll regret it."

"I don't know anything," Dawson protested. He could guess from what little that had been said, but that was all it was. A guess.

"Don't play dumb with me, boy." Burke let go of Dawson's shirt, shoving him backwards.

Dawson stumbled, managing to remain on his feet. He took a step back, his gaze remaining on Burke. "Part of copying something is how much pressure is used. I need to see the originals."

Burke's eyes narrowed. "You better not be lying."

"He told me that too," Levi said.

Burke glared at his son. "Why didn't you tell me earlier?"

Levi took another step away from his father. "Didn't think about it. It was ages ago."

Burke faced Dawson again, taking out his phone. "What's your address? I'll have Levi drop the originals off."

There was no way he was about to give them his address. Did they think he was an idiot? "I'll wait here for him."

"Be about an hour. You might want to rethink that." Burke continued to hold his phone.

Dawson tried not to think about the dinner. It

looked like he'd have to cancel out on it. "I'll be here." Or not. Neither of them knew where he lived and school wouldn't be back in for months. He could ignore Burke's demands and go home once the two of them left.

Burke pointed a finger at him. "You better be here when Levi gets back. Or I will come after you."

Dawson didn't need to ask him to clarify that comment. Even if the words had been unintelligible, he would have understood perfectly from Burke's tone alone. "I'll be here."

Burke returned his phone to his pocket, glancing at his son. "Get a move on." He strode towards the rear exit of the school.

Levi pointed a finger at Dawson. "You better not screw this up. Or I'll be helping him beat the crap out of you."

"You shouldn't have involved me in this." Dawson took a step towards Levi, glaring at him.

Levi stumbled back several steps. "You wouldn't act so tough if you knew how many'd be after you if you screw this up." His lips twisted into a mocking smile. "Guess you should have forged that second note for me." He hurried after his father.

"Good thinking, asking for the originals," Jack said.

"You can take them to the fuzz so they can go after them."

Dawson spun to face Jack. "Who are you? And don't tell me a ghost. That doesn't make sense." He scanned the area. "You must be some sort of hologram or something." He couldn't see anything out of the ordinary so he had no idea how a hologram could have been displayed. Yet there had to be something.

"If I'm a hologram then why didn't Burke and Levi notice me?" Jack asked.

Dawson shrugged. "There has to be a logical explanation. Ghosts don't exist."

Jack chuckled. "So everyone keeps telling me, yet here I am."

Dawson slowly shook his head. "There must be a logical explanation."

"When you figure it out, let me know." Jack nodded in the direction of the groundsman's shed. "But while you're working on that, how about we go back to my place in case they return early."

"Your place?" Dawson walked beside Jack, curious as to what he meant and determined to figure out how he'd done his earlier trick. Not that he was about to leave the school grounds with Jack. The guy was either seriously messed up and believed he was a ghost or was up to something by trying to trick him into believing he was a ghost. "Do you live nearby?" He had enough problems to deal with when it came to Levi and Burke without worrying about Jack. It looked like he was going to be in trouble with the police because there was no way he was about to forge cheques. Especially not ones that took money from old people. He had no grandparents, most of them dead before he'd been born, but that didn't mean he'd prey on someone else's grandparents. Being in trouble for forging a handful of permission slips had to be a lot better than ending up being caught forging cheques.

"I'm not sure you could actually call it living." Jack stopped in front of the closed door of the groundsman's shed. "Give me a moment to unlock it." He walked through the closed door.

Dawson stared at the timber door. There had to be a trick involved. He cautiously reached out a hand to touch the timber. It was solid. When nothing happened, he tried the handle. It was locked. Jack stepped through the closed door again and Dawson stumbled backwards when his hand collided with Jack. He was as solid as the door. "How did you do that? How can you be real yet walk through solid objects?"

"I already told you. I'm a ghost." Jack turned to face the door. "Let me try this again. I don't always get it right first go." Jack strode through the door and it swung open. He looked over his shoulder. "Coming in?"

Again Dawson cautiously stretched out his hand, this time encountering nothing where the door had been. "How did you do that?" He stepped forward when Jack moved out of the doorway, taking out his phone and using the flashlight app to see what the shed contained, half expecting something that belonged on a movie set that would allow Jack to do his tricks.

There was nothing out of the ordinary. Tools, boxes, broken furniture, messy shelves and a wardrobe in the far corner which Jack was stepping through. He hurried after him, determined to figure out the trick. The wardrobe was solid, his hand not going through the timber. Finding a gap at the side, he squeezed past it and into the space behind.

Jack sat on the floor, leaning against the wall, his leg drawn up with his arm resting on it. "Welcome to my place." He made a sweeping gesture with his hand that had been resting on the floor.

Chapter Five

Dawson

"Is this a prank?" Dawson's gaze rested on the handful of items in the space behind the wardrobe. There was a photo of an old motorbike blu tacked to the wall next to a photocopied picture of a smiling girl with blue eyes and blond hair. On the floor was a brown cushion, two phone chargers and a battery powered lantern with a piece of paper under it. Leaning against the wall was a cricket bat, a ball sitting on the floor beside it. Half expecting the piece of paper under the lantern to be some mocking comment about tricking him, Dawson turned on the lantern, slipped his phone in a pocket after he turned off the app and picked up and unfolded the piece of paper. He frowned when he saw it was a website address. Underneath it was written the words 'Jack Richards Fan Club'.

Jack chuckled. "Marti thought it was amusing."

"Who?" He glanced at the picture on the wall. "Is that Marti?"

"No. That's Rose."

Dawson recognised Jack's flat and expressionless tone. He'd used it often enough himself since his parents had died. Rose obviously wasn't a topic up for discussion. That was okay with him as long as Jack answered the other questions he had. "Then who is Marti?"

Jack nodded towards the piece of paper Dawson held. "Do you think you can go on the website and contact her? She should have been here by now. I'm worried something has happened to her."

Dawson looked from the piece of paper to Jack several times, eventually shaking his head. "I don't know what's going on here, but-" He was interrupted by a voice calling out.

"Jack? You home? Sorry I'm late."

Dawson turned to face the gap he'd entered through, about to ask Jack who it was. He stopped when a girl slipped through the gap, grinning when she spotted him. She had sandy brown hair, lots of freckles and would make the perfect model for a pixie. In any other situation he would have asked if he could draw her. Instead, he studied her so he'd be able to draw her later from memory.

"Sorry. I didn't realise anyone else was visiting today." She held out a hand. "I'm Marti."

Dawson looked from Marti to Jack and then back again, not taking the hand he'd been offered and wishing Jack had remained seated. "The one who put together the website?" He held up the piece of paper.

Marti nodded, lowering her hand. "Yes. Which one are you?"

"Tell her you're the latest one," Jack said.

Dawson eyed the gap between the wardrobe and the wall that Marti stood in front of. "You want me to repeat what you said?" He glanced at Jack.

"I want-" Marti's mouth dropped open, a smile slowly forming. "You can hear him? See him? You're the one he's helping now?" She hurried forward and grabbed Dawson's empty hand. "What is he saying?"

Jack chuckled. "Tell her I was worried about her."

Dawson drew his hand from Marti's grip. "What is going on? Are you part of the trick or whatever it is?"

Marti laughed. "Ah, good. I've arrived right at the start. What does he need to help you with? Can I help?"

Dawson looked between the two of them, then gave the piece of paper to Marti. "You're both insane." He pushed past Marti and squeezed out between the wall and the wardrobe.

Marti hurried after him. "Wait. What's your name?"

Dawson ran into the broken furniture as he took his phone out of his pocket and turned on the flashlight app. Night had fallen while he'd been behind the wardrobe and the lantern he'd left on had only given enough light to show him indistinct shadows. "Look, I've got enough problems to deal with-"

Marti interrupted him. "I can help."

Stepping outside, Dawson turned to face her. "I doubt it." He looked her up and down.

"You can say it, everyone else does."

"Say what?"

Marti grinned. "A comment about my size. I've heard them all. So go ahead. Let's see if you can come up with something original."

"He's bigger than me."

"They're always bigger than me. But that doesn't stop me." Marti grinned again. "Is it going to stop you?"

Dawson slowly shook his head. "You know this is insane, right? So either there is something seriously wrong with the two of you or you're trying to play a joke on me. Who put you up to this?"

Marti stepped close to him. "I wish I could help you believe that all of this is true." She grinned. "I know. I'll tell everyone that Jack is helping someone." She stared at the screen of her phone, rapidly tapping away at it.

Dawson peered at the screen. "What is the 'Jack Richards Fan Club' meant to be?"

She didn't answer immediately, waiting until she finished typing and lowering her phone before she spoke. "It's those of us that Jack saved. If it wasn't for him, I'd probably be dead."

He glanced past Marti to the doorway of the groundsman's shed where Jack stood. "You can't seriously expect me to believe you're telling the truth."

Jack pointed at Dawson. "Don't go anywhere."

Dawson started after Jack. "Where are you going?"

"They might be back. Tell Marti to hide in the groundsman's shed and shut the door."

"What do you mean they might be back?" Dawson demanded. "He said he'd be an hour." They hadn't been talking for that long. Not even close.

Marti grabbed Dawson's arm. "What's going on? What's Jack saying?"

Jack grabbed Dawson's arm. "Tell Marti to get inside now." He dragged Dawson into the groundsman's shed.

Chapter Six

Dawson

"Let go of me." Dawson tried to pull away from Jack. He'd had enough. Didn't they realise the problems he had with Burke and Levi were big enough that he didn't need their prank on top of it?

Marti followed them into the groundsman's shed. "What's going on?" She closed the door, plunging the shed into near darkness when she put her phone away.

"Enough–"

Dawson's words were cut off by Jack grabbing him and clamping his hand over his mouth. "Can't you hear someone outside?" Jack demanded.

Dawson started to shake his head, but heard footsteps walking past the shed. He stilled.

Marti moved close to whisper in Dawson's ear. "Is that them outside? Whoever you're trying to avoid."

Jack let Dawson go. "Don't do anything stupid." He strode through the closed door. The sound of it locking was loud in the silence.

Dawson took out his phone, planning to turn on the flashlight app, the light from the lantern doing little to help him see more than indistinct shadows.

Marti grabbed the phone off him before he could turn the flashlight app on. "What are you doing?" She kept her voice low. "Whoever is out there will notice an increase in the light in here."

When a message notification came through, Dawson took the phone back from Marti. The message was from Levi. *Where are you? Thought you said you were going to stay at school.*

Marti peered at the screen. "What are you going to tell them? And you should put your phone on silent so he can't hear it if he tries to ring."

Dawson had no idea what to do. He kept his voice as low as Marti's, setting his phone to silent. "What is really going on? What are you and Jack planning?" If he could at least sort that problem out it'd be one less thing to deal with.

Marti laughed softly. "Poor Jack. No one ever believes him. He is a ghost. And he's stuck here trying to atone for his sins. Mainly that of accidentally shooting his ex, Rose, and her new boyfriend. Did you have a look at the website? It has all sorts of information about him and what he did during his life. Including a forum where you can talk to those of us he's helped."

He stared at her shadow for a moment, wishing he could see her expression. "How can you expect me to believe you? Ghosts don't exist."

"Maybe they don't normally, but Jack exists. Even though I can't see or hear him anymore, I know he exists and is real."

She sounded so sincere. He didn't know her. He'd seen her around school a few times, but she hung out with other people. And he didn't know them either. He was almost relieved when his phone vibrated to notify him of another message. It was from Levi, like he expected. *Dawson! You need to answer me.*

Marti looked up from the screen of the phone. "Dawson?"

"I wish I could believe you." He typed in a message for Levi and sent it. *Have you got what I asked for?*

No. Now where are you?

Let me know when you've got it and I'll catch up with you then.

He's not going to be impressed. He sent me to keep an

eye on you since it'll take longer than he expected to get what you wanted.

Your dad isn't impressed? Dawson was tempted to add that he didn't care what Levi's father thought.

No. Now where are you?

Having dinner. Now quit messaging me until you've got what I asked for.

You don't know who you're messing with.

Then why don't you tell me? Dawson was getting sick of the messages and was tempted to ignore them.

Jack walked through the closed door. "It's that kid who was here before. Levi. He's leaving."

Another message came through on Dawson's phone, saving him having to reply to Jack. *I'm not going to fall for that.* Dawson grinned. He hadn't expected Levi would, but it had been worth a chance. Ignoring the message, he turned on the flashlight app and tried to open the door. It was locked. He turned to Jack. "You going to let me out?"

"If keeping you locked in here would keep you safe, I might consider it." Jack nodded towards the phone Dawson held. "I doubt you'd stay here for long. You'd probably call someone."

"Is Jack in here?" Marti asked.

"You can drop the act," Dawson said. "I'm not

going to fall for it. There has to be a logical explanation."

Marti grinned. "There is a logical explanation. Ghosts exist. And Jack is a ghost."

Turning away from Marti, Dawson gestured towards the door. "Come on, Jack, open the door." If he hurried, he could still make it home in time to go out to dinner with his brother.

"Try not to do anything stupid." Jack stepped through the door and it swung open.

Marti followed Dawson outside. "I'm going with you. If you won't accept Jack's help, I'm willing to offer mine."

Dawson turned on his flashlight app and stopped to face Marti. "You don't even know what's going on. How dangerous it could be." He had a feeling it was life threateningly dangerous. Burke didn't seem like the sort of person to make idle threats.

Marti grinned. "It's okay. It would be nice to repay Jack by helping him keep you alive."

Jack stood beside Dawson, having followed them outside. "You tell Marti that she doesn't owe me anything. I'm glad I could help her."

"Why don't you tell her yourself instead of playing these games?" Dawson was getting sick of the act, or whatever it was. He was fast losing patience with the two of them.

"What did he say?" Marti asked.

Dawson shook his head. "I'm out of here." He strode towards the fence, ignoring the two of them when they followed.

Marti grabbed his arm when he reached the fence. "Please, Dawson. I've been talking to him for months without knowing what he's been saying. One word. That's all I want. Please give me one word from him."

Either she was a really good actor, or she truly believed everything she was telling him. "How can he be a ghost?"

"Tell her I appreciate her spending time with me each week, but she shouldn't feel obligated to," Jack said.

"Please, Dawson." Marti's grip tightened on his arm and the words were soft enough that Dawson leaned towards her to hear them clearly.

He sighed heavily, repeating Jack's last sentence.

Marti threw her arms around Dawson. "Thank you. Thank you so much." She drew away from him, looking around. "Where is he? I want to look at him when I speak to him."

Dawson gestured towards Jack. "There." What if it was true? What if ghosts really existed? Could he somehow talk to his parents? He thought of all the things he'd never had the chance to say to them and the conversations they'd never been able to have.

Marti faced Jack. "Even though I can't hear you, I would never stop visiting you. Without you I wouldn't be alive. You're one of my best friends."

"Thank you, Marti." Jack stepped forward so he was standing directly in front of her. "That means a lot."

Dawson repeated Jack's words.

Marti laughed, her eyes bright with unshed tears that glinted in the light cast by Dawson's phone. "I was beginning to think I'd never get to meet anyone you were helping. It's been so long."

"Tell me about it," Jack said dryly.

Chapter Seven

Dawson

Dawson looked between Jack and Marti. "Maybe the pair of you are telling the truth, but I don't have time to play interpreter. Not if I want to join my brother for dinner." And there were too many things he'd missed out on. Other family dinners and outings he hadn't bothered going to because he'd thought there'd always be another time.

Marti smiled up at Dawson. "I'm coming with you."

"You weren't invited," Dawson said.

Marti's smile didn't dim. "Until you can no longer see Jack, I'm not leaving your side."

Dawson tucked his phone in a pocket and vaulted the fence, taking it out again once he was on the other side. "Not likely."

"Just watch me." Marti also vaulted the fence.

Jack chuckled. "Don't let her size fool you. Her determination and grit make up for her lack of height."

"Great," Dawson muttered.

Marti kept pace with Dawson, almost running to keep up with his stride. "What did he say?"

Dawson glanced at Marti. "That you're a pain."

She laughed. "No, really. What did he say?"

Dawson shook his head. "You can't come with me. That's not the way this is done."

"The way what is done?" Marti asked.

He glanced at her again. "Dinner. End of school year celebration dinner."

"Your brother takes you out to dinner at the end of the school year?"

He started to nod, but it felt like it would have been a lie. This was the first time his brother would be taking him out to dinner. "Our parents used to."

"Why can't they do it this time?"

"They're dead." His voice was flat and expressionless. Any other tone and people usually asked questions.

Marti placed her hand on his arm. "I'm sorry. I lost my grandfather. I know how hard it is to lose someone you love. I can't imagine how painful it must be to lose two at once."

"It was years ago."

She smiled up at him, a hint of sadness to it, her hand still resting on his arm. "It doesn't matter how much time has passed. It always hurts."

He stopped under the next streetlight to turn and face her. He could see the sorrow in her eyes. "I'm sorry about your grandfather."

Her hand, which still rested on his arm, momentarily tightened. "Thank you."

"Can Jack contact others who've died? Like your grandfather." He paused. "Or my parents."

She shook her head. "No. It doesn't work like that. I'd hoped it meant I could talk to my grandfather too." A wistful smile briefly formed. "If there are other ghosts, I don't know of their existence and I've never seen another one other than Jack. I only saw him for three days. And they weren't even three full days."

"How did he convince you he was a ghost?"

Marti laughed. "I pushed my motorbike through him."

"You have a motorbike licence? I didn't think you were old enough."

"I'm not. And I don't. At least not yet. It's a long

story and right now we should be focused on sorting out your problems."

Dawson shrugged, stepping back from her so her hand fell from his arm. "They don't know where I live so all I have to do is stay out of their way and it won't be a problem. They want me to forge cheques to steal money from old people."

"You're not going to do it, are you?"

He shook his head. "Absolutely not. I might forge the occasional permission slip, and sick note to take time off school, but that's it."

"Good. I hate people who prey on the elderly. If anyone had tried something like that on my grandad…" Her voice trailed off threateningly and her hands curled into fists.

"I don't have grandparents, but I-" Dawson broke off when he caught sight of Levi striding towards them.

"What's wrong?" Marti asked.

Levi reached them before Dawson could say anything. "Where do you think you're going?"

"I already told you. Dinner." Dawson stepped between Marti and Levi.

"With your girlfriend?" Levi glanced past Dawson.

Marti stepped around Dawson so she stood at his side. "What's it got to do with you?"

"Stay out of it." Levi barely glanced at Marti before returning his attention to Dawson. "I already told you what's happening tonight. And it doesn't include anyone else."

Dawson had no idea what to do. He really wanted to join his brother for dinner. It wouldn't be the same as having their parents there, but it was the closest he could get to having them celebrate the end of the school year with him.

"I hope he's not a friend." Marti looked Levi up and down.

"Not even close," Dawson said. "He's one of those people you hate."

"Good." Marti grinned as she took a step forward. "Leave us alone. You won't like what I do if you don't."

Levi stared at her for a moment before he burst out laughing. "I'm so scared." His tone was filled with sarcasm as he continued to grin at her.

Marti slowly shook her head. "They always underestimate me." Taking another step forward, she kneed Levi, bringing him to the ground. Turning, she grabbed Dawson's hand, dragging him with her when she broke into a run.

Dawson glanced over his shoulder several times, wincing when he saw Levi remained on the ground, swearing and complaining. "I won't be making that mistake."

Marti laughed, dragging him down the side of someone's house. "I bet he won't either."

"Where are you heading?"

"There's a bus stop a couple of streets over. We can cut through some yards that don't have pets and be there in minutes."

Dawson's phone rang and checking it, he saw it was his brother. He'd obviously not made it home in time. He answered the call. "Can I meet you there?"

"You're meant to leave a message so I know where you are. The drawing you left on the kitchen table doesn't count. Unless you were letting me know you were off to fight the hounds of hell with your demon companion."

A smile formed. "Sorry. And you've got it wrong. I'm fighting demons with my hell hound companion." He slowed, checking both ways before running across the road with Marti. "So, how about it? Can I meet you at the restaurant?"

"Where are you? I can pick you up."

Dawson glanced at Marti. "With a mate. Can she come to dinner too?"

"I can pay my way," Marti offered.

"A mate."

Dawson grinned at his brother's tone. "Yes, a mate." He paused a moment. "What's your answer?"

Morgan didn't answer immediately and before he did, he sighed heavily. "Okay. And don't you break any of your promises."

Dawson tried not to think of Levi and Burke. "I'm trying to keep them."

"That doesn't sound good. What did you do?"

"Nothing." At least he'd done nothing this time. The opposite in fact.

Once again there was a pause and another sigh before Morgan spoke. "I hope not." There was another pause. "I'll meet you at the restaurant."

"Okay. See you soon." After disconnecting, Dawson slipped the phone into a pocket of his jeans, slowing to a stop as they reached the bus shelter. He'd noticed a couple of missed messages, but he wasn't interested in what Levi had to say.

Chapter Eight

Dawson

It took Dawson two buses and nearly half an hour before they reached the restaurant, a small family one up the road from a shopping complex. Morgan, who was parked out the front, got out of his car as they approached.

Dawson introduced Marti to Morgan, somehow managing not to keep checking over his shoulder to make sure Levi hadn't found them. He also ignored the many vibrations notifying him of messages, tempted to turn his phone off.

Morgan nodded in greeting, gesturing towards the restaurant. "Are we ready to go in before it gets too busy and we have to wait ages for a table?"

Marti grinned. "I'm starving."

Dawson followed his brother inside, Marti beside

him. She leaned close to him while Morgan was busy requesting a table.

"We should go to the police."

"And tell them what? I know next to nothing." Dawson stepped away from her when his brother turned to face them.

"They just have to finish clearing a table before they can seat us."

The three of them remained silent as they waited for a table, Marti the one breaking the silence once they were seated. She picked up one of the menus in the centre of the table. "What's good here?"

"Everything, we usually get a pizza to celebrate the end of school," Dawson said. Or at least that's what his parents had always ordered for them. Something they all enjoyed.

Marti glanced at the menu once more before returning it to the centre of the table. "Sounds good to me."

"Anything you won't eat on a pizza?" Morgan asked.

Marti shook her head. "The more toppings, the better."

Silence fell again and Dawson tried to think of something to say to break it. All he could think of was Burke's demands. He couldn't afford to have any of the permission slips he'd handed in during the last few years be scrutinised. He didn't want to think about the sort of trouble he'd end up in. But it would probably come to a point where he'd have to admit what he'd done or end up doing something worse.

After a waiter had taken their orders, Marti glanced around the restaurant. "I didn't know this place existed. It's not that far from home."

"Are you new to the area?" Morgan asked.

Marti shook her head then glanced at Dawson. "We go to the same school." The conversation turned to teachers, classes and various other school related topics. It carried them through the meal and part of the way through dessert where the conversation turned to plans for the holidays.

Morgan shook his head in answer to Marti's question. "We won't be going anywhere for the holidays. I'll be working right up till Christmas. It was the only way I could get Christmas day off."

Finished her ice cream, Marti set the spoon back in the bowl. "At least you get Christmas off." She pushed the bowl away from her. "There's a group of us getting together to celebrate the end of the school year tonight and we're all going to crash at my place afterwards. Can Dawson join us?"

"I'm not sure–"

Dawson interrupted his brother. He wanted to speak to Jack again and figure out what to do. It seemed wrong to let Burke continue to rip people off. Even if all he did was tell the police what was going on. "It's the end of the school year. It's not like I have to be up early or anything."

"Well… " Morgan drew the word out.

"There won't be any alcohol," Marti said. "My mum wouldn't allow that."

"I suppose-" Morgan began.

"Thank you," Marti exclaimed. "He should be home by midday tomorrow, late afternoon at the most."

Morgan checked his phone. "Do you want a lift? I should have enough time before I have to pick Cleo up. We're going to a late movie."

Dawson shook his head. "It's okay. We can catch a bus."

"Are you sure?" Morgan eyed him up and down, suspicion in his tone.

Dawson grinned. "Aren't you the one who complains you don't get to see your girlfriend enough with the amount of hours you work? As if I'd cut into that time."

Morgan laughed, rising to his feet. "Okay. Fair

enough." When they headed outside, Morgan took Dawson aside. "Don't forget your promises."

"You don't have to keep reminding me." Guilt struck him. He would have to tell his brother about the forgeries. Eventually. After he told the police.

Morgan glanced over at Marti. "I'm glad you're hanging out with friends again."

Dawson shrugged, feeling more guilty about his brother having the wrong idea over that than keeping him in the dark about Burke. Especially since his brother had kept fighting to have him move in with him.

Morgan studied him for a moment. "Are you sure there's nothing you want to tell me?"

"I'm sure." Dawson took half a step towards Marti. "Can I go now? Before the party is over?"

Morgan sighed. "Yeah. Just try and stay out of trouble."

Dawson bit back the sarcastic comment he wanted to make. He supposed his brother did have a reason to worry. "I'll see you tomorrow." He walked with Marti towards the bus stop, glancing over his shoulder to see his brother remained by his car, leaning against it as he watched them leave.

Marti linked her arm through Dawson's. "Did you want to tell him?"

"Absolutely not." He dreaded to think how his brother would react when he found out. He'd have to tell him eventually, but not yet.

"You should ring the police and let them know. Surely they can help," Marti suggested. "Although I really want to ask you to return to Jack first so you can pass along a few more messages for me before he disappears, but that wouldn't be right. It might put you in more danger."

A bus pulled up and Dawson checked where it was headed before boarding, glancing towards where his brother had been parked. He was gone.

Marti tugged Dawson to the back of the bus once they'd paid their fare. No one was in the last few rows and she tilted her head towards him before she spoke. "You probably don't want to catch up with Levi again. I think he's going to be pretty unhappy with us."

Dawson chuckled. "That's an understatement." He glanced at the other people on the bus, none of them close enough to hear them. "What did you mean about visiting Jack first?"

"Once you're safe, he'll disappear and you'll never get to see or speak to him again."

"Why?"

She shrugged. "It's just how it works."

He didn't know how he felt about that. Although it wasn't like he really knew the ghost. He thought of the flat tone Jack had used when he'd said Rose's name. He might not know him, but he could relate to the pain that came with not wanting to talk about someone he'd lost. And Marti obviously knew him and wanted to know what he had to say. "I can wait."

Marti shook her head. "No. Jack only ever appears for people in danger. People who might die. At least that's what we've figured out between us."

Chapter Nine

Dawson

Shock arrowed through Dawson. He could die? He thought of his brother leaning against his car, watching him walk away. He couldn't do that to him. Not with all he'd gone through to get him away from their aunt and uncle. Taking out his phone, he stared at it for a moment before he looked up the number for the local police station. He was put on hold several times when he said he wanted to report a crime. He missed the name the next person gave when he answered, but decided it probably wasn't worth asking as he'd only hand him on to someone else. "I need to report a crime."

"When did it occur?"

"Ah, well, I'm not sure." It wasn't like Burke had told him much. Levi had told him more than his father had with his comment about old people using cheques.

"What is the crime then?"

He nearly hung up at the sound of annoyance he heard in the man's voice. "Forging cheques."

There was a moment of silence before the man spoke again. "Have you reported it to your bank?"

"They're not my cheques."

"So you haven't contacted the bank. What have you done then?"

"Ah…" Dawson was momentarily lost for words. Other than not wanting to forge a cheque, he hadn't done anything.

"If this is some kind of end of school year joke–"

Dawson interrupted the man. "No, I wouldn't do that."

"Are you sure this isn't something to do because you missed out on going to schoolies or some such thing?" the man demanded.

"No, I–"

The man interrupted Dawson. "Put one of your parents on the phone."

"I can't. They're dead." He disconnected the call, lowering his phone. He should have known he was wasting his time. When was the last time anyone had believed anything he'd said? Other than his brother who regularly doubted him when it came to keeping out of trouble.

Marti rested her hand on his arm. "We'll work something out."

He nodded, even though he wasn't sure what could be done. He thought of all the missed messages, but couldn't face reading them just yet.

They remained silent, needing to change buses once to return to the school. This time they exited on the other side of the school grounds, several streets away. Dawson looked in every direction. The area was clear. Or at least clear of Levi and his father. Checking his phone, he saw a long string of missed messages from Levi. Again he couldn't bring himself to read them.

Marti grabbed his hand. "This way." She led him through several yards, pausing across the road from the school grounds. "We should go further along that way so we can avoid the lights. Just in case there's someone watching for us."

Dawson drew away from her. "You wait here and I'll see if anyone is about."

"You don't have–" Marti broke off when Dawson's phone vibrated and the screen lit up. She laughed, the sound awkward, her hand pressed against her chest. "I wasn't expecting that."

Dawson decline the call when he saw it was Levi. The phone vibrated again almost straight away, notifying him that Levi was trying to ring him again.

"I don't think he's going to stop."

Dawson answered the call. "What?"

"You better check your last message."

"Stop ringing me," Dawson ordered.

Levi laughed. "You're the one who'll ring me when you see your last message." He disconnected the call.

Dawson doubted it, but he checked anyway, staring at the picture Levi had sent. Fear washed over him and his first reaction was to go home and check that everything was okay.

Marti peered at the screen of his phone. "Whose house?"

"Mine. It's where my brother and I live."

"Levi sent it to you?"

Dawson nodded, his hand tightening on his phone. He wished now that he'd kicked Levi when he was down. Several times. This could only be a threat. Against him and his brother. Fear rushed through him. What if Morgan had gone home first? He dialled his brother's number.

"This better be good. We're about to go into the movie."

For a moment he wasn't able to speak. "It can wait until tomorrow." He was surprised his voice sounded so normal. "It wasn't anything important."

"You sure?"

"Yeah." He paused a moment. "Enjoy the movie." That didn't give him much time to sort this out.

"I will. See you tomorrow. I'll be staying at Cleo's tonight if you need me."

He tried to keep the relief he felt out of his voice. "Okay. See you then." Disconnecting the call, he stared down at his phone. "I don't want to forge cheques for them." But he also didn't want anything to happen to his brother.

"Then we find a way to prove what they're doing and who's involved." Marti took out her phone and accessed the forum on the website.

"What are you doing?"

"Leaving my phone number and checking what everyone had to say about my earlier message." She looked up at him with a grin. "They're all interested in helping. Just waiting to be told how they can help."

"Why would they risk their lives for me?" Dawson asked.

Marti received a notification on her phone, smiling as she read it over. "It's Aiden. He's left the Gold

Coast and will be here in about an hour and a half." She tilted the phone so he could see the message. "He said it's the last day of schoolies and he'd have been heading back tomorrow anyway."

"Who is Aiden?"

"Jack helped him." Marti checked the second message. "Jena said she'll meet us at the groundsman's shed."

"Tell her we don't know who's around and that we're across the road from it." He slowly shook his head. "You might get hurt. All of you might end up hurt." He glanced down at the picture of his house. They obviously were serious. And he needed to call Levi to find out what they planned to do.

Marti looked up from her phone, having replied to the messages. "So might you, but between all of us, we should be able to work something out." She'd barely finished speaking when another message came through. "It's from Lucy. She asked if you needed help."

"Tell her there are enough of you risking your lives," Dawson said.

Marti's fingers moved across the screen of her phone, typing in a message. "I'll tell her who's coming and let her make up her own mind."

"This is insane." Dawson looked in the direction of

the school. "It's not just Levi. It's his father too. And who knows how many others are involved."

"Then it's a good thing we've got reinforcements coming." Marti slipped her phone in a pocket and took his from him.

He started to protest.

"I'll give you my number in case you need to call or message me." She sent herself a message from his phone, smiling when she handed his phone back and checked her own, saving his number. "Now we have to figure out how to prove to the police what Levi and his father are up to."

Chapter Ten

Dawson

Dawson tried to think of something he could say to convince Marti of how dangerous it was to help him. She might have brought Levi down, but Burke wouldn't be so easily dealt with. Movement caught his attention. He turned to see a girl around his age riding towards him on a bicycle. She slowed as she approached, stopping well back from them. She had medium brown hair, tied back in a ponytail and her brown eyes darted between them, filled with worry.

"I'm Marti." She gestured to the side. "And this is Dawson."

"I'm Jena." She laughed softly. "When I saw the two of you I realised I didn't know what you looked like." She laughed again. "Then I started thinking of all these crazy scenarios. With serial killers and murders."

Marti grinned. "I should send the others a pic of us so they can recognise who we are." She dragged Dawson with her, standing beside Jena.

Once again, Dawson felt like he should protest. Things like this didn't happen to him. No one ever put themselves out to help him. Let alone were willing to risk their lives for him.

Before Marti could take a photo, another message came through on her phone. "Lucy's on the way." With a grin, she took their picture.

Jena blinked repeatedly when the flashlight went off, her eyes remaining closed for several seconds. "What can I do to help?"

"We don't know if it's safe to head over there." Marti gestured in the direction of the school grounds.

Dawson stepped between Jena and the school grounds. "No. You're not going over there alone. Anyone could be over there."

Jena shifted so she could study the school grounds. "If you can get close enough, Jack could tell you if anyone is about."

"You need to talk to Levi," Marti said. "You need to find out all the information you can so you can convince the police about what's going on."

Dawson opened his mouth to speak, closing it when there was another notification on Marti's phone. He checked the screen when she did, nearly groaning when he read the message. "We don't need more help."

"Of course we do." Marti grinned at him. "Besides, Kobe and Xavier are on their way. I'll just let them know where we are."

"I think you're enjoying this a little too much." Dawson waited for Marti to look up from the screen of her phone before he continued. "This is dangerous. Burke is dangerous." Levi probably not so much, but who knew what he'd be willing to do if his father ordered it.

"All the more reason for us to make sure Burke goes to prison." Marti returned her phone to her pocket.

"What exactly is going on?" Jena asked. "Maybe I can help come up with a solution."

At a noise, they all turned to watch a girl walk towards them.

"I'm Lucy." She smiled at each of them. "You can't imagine how happy I am to meet all of you." She faced Dawson. "I guess you're the one who can see Jack."

Dawson nodded. The curvaceous girl had blue

eyes, chestnut coloured hair falling past her shoulders and, like the rest of them, wore jeans and a t-shirt.

"Can you give him a message from me?" Lucy asked

Jena hopped off her bicycle. "And one from me too?"

Dawson didn't get the chance to say anything before two boys joined them, striding along the footpath to stop in front of him. He shook hands with the one who'd been in the lead, feeling once again like he should protest. "I'm Dawson." He wasn't sure when he'd lost control of the situation, but Jack had been right. Marti's determination and grit certainly made up for her lack of height.

"I'm Kobe and this is Xavier."

"You really didn't have to come." Dawson studied each of the boys. Kobe had sandy brown hair, hazel eyes and a narrow jaw while Xavier had dark hair, brown eyes and a solid build.

"Well, if you don't need us…" Xavier took a step back.

Kobe grabbed hold of his arm and drew him forward again. "Of course they need us." He turned to Dawson again. "What's the problem? If we're going to help you come up with a plan, we need more details."

Dawson looked at each of them, his protests dying before he started making them. None of them looked like they'd be easily dissuaded. "I don't know much, just that Levi and his father are involved in forging cheques." He went over all the details he knew, finishing with a glance towards the school. "And I need to find out if there's anyone who'll prevent me from going over to talk to Jack before I return Levi's phone call and find out why he sent me a picture of my house."

"That one's easy," Jena said. "It's a threat. They know where you live."

"We can check who's at the school," Kobe offered at that same time as Lucy spoke.

"I can see if anyone is over there."

Kobe gave a single nod. "That's settled then. The three of us will see who's at the school while the rest of you figure out an excuse as to why Dawson can't meet up with Levi and why he took so long to ring back."

Jena spoke as the three left. "I know the perfect excuse. You're at an end of school party trying to find a lift back here."

"If he suggests organising a lift for you, tell him you're not about to let him know where your friends live," Marti said.

Nodding, Dawson rang Levi, putting it on speaker.

He answered on the first ring. "You really don't want to go upsetting anyone. It's a really bad idea."

"This is all your fault. You should have kept your mouth shut," Dawson said.

"Guess you should have been nicer to me."

Before Dawson could argue the comment, Levi spoke again.

"Where are you? I've got the items you wanted."

"At a party. I went there after dinner. There are parties going all weekend to celebrate the end of the school year. I've been trying to get a lift back to the school."

"Where exactly? Dad can pick you up."

"I'm not about to tell you where my friends live. I'm not stupid."

Marti grinned at Dawson's words.

"This better not take all night," Levi warned. "I've got better things to do than wait around for you."

Dawson glared at the phone. He was pretty sure Levi was enjoying bossing him around a little too much. "I'll be there when I get there. I'm not about to risk anyone else."

"Then you should remember that. Haven't you got a brother?" Levi asked.

Chapter Eleven

Dawson

Anger rushed through Dawson and he tightened his grip on his phone.

Marti rested her hand on Dawson's arm, moving closer to him.

Jena moved closer to his other side, smiling reassuringly at him.

Some of Dawson's anger eased. He wasn't alone. He thought of Jack, waiting at the school for him. "I'll ring you when I get a lift."

"One hour," Levi warned.

"I'll let you know." Dawson disconnected the call, glaring at his screen when a message came through.

One hour.

"I've never liked him," Marti said.

"Neither have I," Jena added.

Dawson put his phone away. "Thanks."

"An hour will give Aiden enough time to get here." Marti looked from Jena to Dawson, smiling. "Which will mean all of us that Jack has helped will be here."

Dawson frowned. "Is there an Aiden at our school?"

"I don't know." Marti shrugged. "If there is, they aren't our Aiden. He nearly went to our school, but didn't end up moving." She checked her phone when a message came through. "School is clear."

"We should all exchange numbers," Jena suggested.

After they exchanged numbers, Marti giving them the numbers for the others and passing their numbers along, they headed to the groundsman's shed. Dawson stopped out the front of the shed, facing Jack. It was still hard to believe he could talk to a ghost. "We need to find a way to stop them ripping off the elderly."

"We?" Jack glanced around the area, most of them holding phones with flashlight apps turned on.

"You too, Jack," Dawson said.

Marti faced the same direction as Dawson. "He's here?"

Dawson nodded.

"Aiden is on his way." Marti looked at each of them, grinning. "We'll all be together soon."

"Just like she wanted." Jack's gaze rested on Marti.

Dawson repeated Jack's words.

Marti nodded. "Between us, I'm sure we can figure out a way to put them in jail."

"We should go inside, in case one of them turns up," Jena said.

Jack walked through the door, unlocking it. Dawson followed him inside, the rest of them following him.

Kobe chuckled. "We're not all going to fit behind the wardrobe."

Dawson waited until they were all inside then closed the door. "Here will do." He checked the time. "We don't have long to figure something out before I need to ring Levi."

They all spoke at once, some laughing, others smiling, all of them falling quiet. Jack spoke when it was silent. "Have you warned them how dangerous this is?"

Dawson nodded. "Yeah, they know." At the questioning looks, he added, "How dangerous this is."

"I'm not about to let someone's grandparent be preyed upon," Marti stated, the others agreeing with her.

"So what's the plan then?" Xavier asked.

They threw ideas back and forth, still discussing

things when Aiden arrived, stepping inside the groundsman's shed and bringing silence, followed by laughter. Dawson looked him over, feeling like he should apologise that he'd cut his night short. He had short black hair, brown eyes and a charismatic smile that Dawson would have liked to capture on paper.

Marti stepped forward. "Come and join us. We're just figuring out what to do. Have you got any suggestions?"

"Sorry I took so long." Aiden turned off his flashlight app. "What ideas have you come up with so far?"

By the time they came up with a plan, it was fifteen minutes after Levi had said Dawson was to meet up with him. Jack searched the school grounds before each of them hid in a location where they could record what would happen. Dawson waited until everyone sent him a message to let him know they were in place before he stepped outside the shed and messaged Levi. *At school. In front of the groundsman's shed.* From what had happened earlier, he assumed they wouldn't stay around the shed, but Marti was nearby in case they did.

Meet you in the place where we were before.

Dawson smiled. Like he'd expected. Levi wasn't very original. He made his way to the classroom,

Jack at his side. He couldn't help thinking of what Marti had said about Jack accidentally shooting his ex girlfriend. "Do you regret it?"

"Regret what?"

It took him a second to remember her name. He could clearly remember what she'd looked like. "Rose."

Jack glanced towards him. "Every single second."

He could hear the regret in Jack's voice. Having no idea what to say, and preferring not to focus on his own regrets, he fell silent, not speaking again until they neared the classroom. "Can you see Levi anywhere yet?"

"No. I'll check on everyone and see that Marti made it to her new location." Jack strode towards the rear exit of the school grounds, the direction Levi and Burke had taken last time.

Dawson remained at the front of the classroom, regularly checking his phone. There were no messages. He wanted to send messages to all the others to make sure they were okay. But Jack was checking on them and would be back soon. He hoped. A noise drew Dawson's attention.

Jack strode ahead of Levi, reaching Dawson not long before him. "I didn't get a chance to check on anyone. Levi was already on his way."

"Where's your dad?" Dawson barely glanced at Jack, wishing he could tell him to check now.

"He'll be here soon." Levi held out a paper bag that seemed to have come from a bottle shop. "He said to give you this and for you to get started."

Chapter Twelve

Dawson

Dawson took the bag from Levi and looked inside. It was a half used chequebook, several pieces of blank paper, some pens and a couple of letters written in cursive writing. "I want to talk to your dad first."

"I'll be back in a minute," Jack said. "I'll check on Marti and Kobe."

Dawson nearly nodded, preventing himself at the last second. He glanced at Levi's phone that he held. "Contact him and tell him I want to talk to him."

"I think you're forgetting we know where you live," Levi said.

For a moment Dawson wondered if he was insane. If he forged the cheque and it was close, but not close enough, there was a good chance they'd leave him alone and not hassle him again. That they'd think him incapable of the job. It took him a second to decide he couldn't ignore what was going on. He'd forged a few permission slips over the years, but nothing that would cause serious harm or hardship to anyone. "You're wasting time. Call your dad."

After another glare at him, Levi snatched the paper bag back from Dawson and dialled his father's number. "He's refusing to help."

Dawson grabbed the phone off Levi, turning his shoulder to him when he tried to take it back. He interrupted Burke. "I haven't refused to help. I said I want to talk to you. In person."

"You're not in a position to make demands."

"Oh, I think I am. This time, I have a proposition for you."

Burke didn't speak immediately. "I'm listening."

"You might be, but I'm not going to discuss this over the phone. And you'd probably prefer that I didn't."

"I'll be there in twenty. Put Levi back on the phone."

"I'll see you then." Dawson held the phone out to Levi who snatched it from him. He grinned when Levi walked several metres away, keeping his back to him, before he spoke too quietly to be heard from where Dawson stood. He started to take a step towards Levi when he saw Jack approaching. He took several steps backwards instead. "Everyone okay?" He whispered the words, barely moving his lips, his gaze remaining on Levi.

Jack nodded. "Both Marti and Kobe are recording. From different angles. You will have to get him to admit what's going on when he turns up."

He didn't bother pointing out that they also needed some proof. His gaze was drawn to the paper bag Levi held. He didn't know if that would be enough proof. It would be a start though.

Levi slipped the phone into his pocket as he turned to face Dawson. "You better hope you've got a good reason for demanding that Dad meet up with you. He'll beat the crap out of you if you're just trying to get out of helping."

Dawson studied Levi. He looked a little too happy with that idea. "Sorry to disappoint you. That's not why I said I needed to see him."

"Why then?" Levi demanded.

Dawson smiled. "You're just going to have to wait to find out."

"Do you think it's a good idea to torment Levi like that?" Jack asked.

Dawson's smile turned into a grin. It might not be, but it was a lot of fun. Especially after all the headaches Levi had caused him and the threats against him and his brother.

Levi spun, stalking away several metres, standing with his arms crossed over his chest. He regularly glanced over his shoulder at Dawson, eyes narrowed.

Dawson scanned the area. Would Burke really only take twenty minutes? Or was that just a phrase he liked to use? He checked the time. Twenty minutes weren't up yet. He checked again five minutes later. There was still no sign of him.

"Stop checking the time," Jack said. "Levi stares at you each time you do instead of the glance he normally gives you when he checks what you're doing."

Dawson resisted the urge to check the time once more. It wasn't until Burke arrived that he finally let himself look at it again. Half an hour was nearly up. He managed not to comment on it when Burke stopped in front of him, a hand tucked into a pocket of his jeans.

"Well?" Burke demanded.

Dawson tried to remain calm. Or at least not let Burke see how terrified he was. The man's broad shoulders and height would give him an advantage in a fight between them. And Burke probably had a better idea how to fight than he did. "Why should

I forge the cheques without getting anything in return?"

"You are getting something in return," Burke said. "You and your brother will get to live."

"I want more than that." He was surprised at how calm he sounded. "A lot more. I have one year left of school before I need to find a job. You can ask Levi. My grades aren't anything exciting and there's no chance of Uni. So what you've got planned looks like a pretty good opportunity to me."

Burke looked him up and down several times before he spoke. "You want in on the action."

Dawson nodded even though it had sounded more like a statement than a question.

Again Burke looked him up and down. "Why do you think I'd believe you'd have such a major change of heart?"

"I haven't had a change of heart at all," Dawson said. "I just couldn't see what was in it for me. Now I can. Which is why I want in. How much could I make in a week? A couple of hundred? Or could I make enough to pay all my expenses so I can focus on my art and not have to get some boring job?"

"You're serious." Burke studied him carefully. "You actually might be serious."

Dawson shrugged. "I had time to think about it

while I was looking for a lift back here. I don't want to spend my days flipping burgers at Maccas. I mean, who would." He managed to keep his expression neutral when all he wanted to do was cheer excitedly at how interested Burke now looked. He needed to be careful not to overdo things.

Burke gestured Levi forward, taking the paper bag from him. "Let's see how well you do with this first. Then we can talk opportunities."

"Give me half an hour. I've copied a similar style of writing to this before." He took the paper bag. "I shouldn't need more than that. How much do you want the cheque made out for?"

"Five hundred. Make it out to cash. That's an average amount that is often drawn on the account every month or two and shouldn't set off any alarms. There should also be enough in the account to cover it according to what is written on the stubs." Burke turned to Levi. "You stay here. I'll be back in twenty."

Chapter Thirteen

Dawson

Dawson waited until Burke strode out of sight before he headed towards one of the tables on the school grounds provided for students to eat their lunch at.

"Where do you think you're going?" Levi hurried after him.

"I'm not about to sit on the ground while I'm copying the handwriting."

"There's a closer one in the other direction," Levi said.

Dawson shrugged. "The one in this direction is well away from the perimeter of the school and any of the security lights." He continued in the same direction.

"I don't trust you," Levi warned.

Dawson shrugged again. "Not my problem." He

sat at the timber and concrete table and bench seat that were cemented into the ground, tipping the contents of the bag onto the table. He angled his phone so the light from it landed on the space in front of him.

"You better not do anything." Levi sat across from him. "I'm watching you."

"That's going to be pretty boring for you." He studied the handwriting, his gaze drawn to the name. Anita. It felt as if someone had punched him. The woman had the same name as his mother. His grip tightened on the pen, the plastic creaking in protest. He couldn't do it. Thoughts of his brother silenced his protests. If everything went right, Anita Gray wouldn't lose a cent and his brother would be safe.

"How long are you going to stare at everything? Thought you said you'd only need half an hour," Levi said.

Dawson pushed everything from his mind except for the writing he needed to copy. He wasn't in this alone. Between all of them they should be able to get all the proof they needed to make sure Burke ended up in jail. He did some practice words on the blank paper before opening up the chequebook. He stared at the figure on the final stub. Just over four thousand dollars. Five hundred dollars was a lot of money when you had little more than four grand. Again he reminded himself that no one would cash the cheque. He'd make sure of it.

"What's taking you so long?" Levi demanded. "Dad will be back soon and you haven't even started."

Dawson didn't bother pointing out that he had started, just hadn't written on one of the cheques. He stared at the blank spaces a moment before he started filling them in, not doing the signature until he'd practiced it a few times on the blank paper. He was just finishing the signature when Burke arrived, standing over him as he waited. He leaned back when Burke grabbed the chequebook. He nearly grabbed it back, not wanting to think about what would happen if something went wrong. To start with, Anita Gray would be down five hundred dollars. Money she probably couldn't afford to lose judging by what she had in her account.

"Not bad," Burke said. "How many do you think you can manage in a day?"

Dawson rose to his feet, picking up his phone and turning off the app since Levi was using his. He slipped it back in his pocket. "Four or five." He shrugged. "Depends on how hard the writing is to copy. Some are easier than others."

"Twenty dollars a cheque," Burke offered.

"Five percent," Dawson said.

"Some cheques are only worth a hundred dollars. Twenty is more than fair considering how many need to be paid." Burke returned the chequebook to the paper bag.

"What about if a cheque is worth a grand? I want five percent." He tried to keep his gaze off the paper bag. He didn't want to let Burke know how interested he was in where the chequebook was put.

"You don't realise how many are involved in making this possible. Twenty dollars is generous."

"Then how about you tell me."

"Someone has to steal the chequebooks, someone needs to cash them in, someone has to write out the cheques and of course someone has to organise everything," Burke said. "So be grateful you're being offered twenty."

"That's only four people. Someone's getting paid better than everyone else." Movement caught his attention and he glanced towards it, noticing Jack coming in close.

"That's none of your business."

"Fine, but that doesn't change that I want five percent," Dawson said. "So what's your answer?"

"I can't give you an answer. That's up to someone else," Burke said.

"Then ring them," Dawson said.

"We don't do business over the phone." Burke glanced in the direction he'd come from. "I can take you to meet him though."

"As if I'd go anywhere with you. Who knows where you'd take me." Dawson crossed his arms over his chest. "Why can't we meet here?"

Burke's eyes narrowed. "You're a little too fond of this school."

Dawson shrugged a single shoulder, his arms remaining crossed over his chest. "It's a public place. That isn't busy and is out of the way. Yet close enough to help if I need it."

Burke grinned. "You think you could make it to help in time if I did something about how annoying you are?"

Dawson remained where he was even though Burke's grin sent a shiver down his spine. "At least I know this area."

Burke looked from Dawson to Levi and back again. "Stay here. I'll be back in twenty."

Dawson tried not to look at the paper bag Burke took with him. The bag that contained proof of what was going on. He only hoped Aiden and Lucy would be able to follow Burke, like they'd planned, if he didn't stick around. Jack strode after Burke so he supposed he'd soon know if they managed to follow him.

Levi glared at Dawson, waiting until his father was out of hearing before he spoke. "I've got better things to do on a Saturday night than babysit you."

Dawson couldn't resist grinning. "Good. Think I didn't have plans?"

Levi took a step towards Dawson. "You better watch out."

He uncrossed his arms. "Or what?" He took a step towards Levi who took several back. "That's what I thought."

Jack strode back towards them. "They managed to follow without being seen. Burke was alone and he put the paper bag on the front seat. You might want to let Aiden know in case they can get it back from him."

Dawson took out his phone, sending the message to Aiden.

"Who are you contacting?" Levi demanded.

"Friends. I didn't expect to be here this long. They were going to pick me up." He lowered his phone. "I didn't think you'd want anyone else turning up here."

"Bad enough I've got to put up with you," Levi muttered.

Dawson checked the message that came through.

This is Lucy. Aiden is driving. We'll try to get the chequebook back.

"Now what?" Levi demanded. "Show me what you're talking about."

"They wanted to know how much longer. Not that it's any of your business." He sent a message thanking Aiden and Lucy. About to put his phone away, another message came through. He grinned when he saw it was a video from Marti, who also let him know Kobe could send him one too.

"Now what is going on?" Levi demanded.

After thanking Marti, Dawson slipped his phone into his pocket since Levi still had his flashlight app turned on. "Feeling jealous that your friends don't contact you?" He grinned at the daggered look Levi sent him.

"Stop messing with him," Jack said. "Even a rat will eventually attack if you poke it enough times."

Chapter Fourteen

Dawson

Dawson laughed, glancing around the area in the hope of finding something to do. He thought of Jack's ability to unlock doors. Taking out his phone again, he typed in a message and tilted his phone so Jack could see it. *Can you unlock the door to the art room?*

Jack peered over Dawson's shoulder. "Why do you want it unlocked?"

Again Dawson used his phone. *For something to do while I wait.*

"Probably better than letting you stir Levi." Jack strode in the direction of the art room.

Dawson turned on the flashlight app before he followed him.

Levi hurried after Dawson, speaking before he

came alongside him. "Where do you think you're going?"

"Guess you'll have to come with me if you want to find out."

Jack glanced over his shoulder. "You might want to slow down so I can get it open before you reach it. Less questions that way."

Dawson slowed his pace, letting Jack get well ahead. He supposed Jack was right. As fun as it might be to confuse Levi about how the door opened, he didn't want to cause problems for Jack.

When they reached the room, the door was open and Levi hurried ahead to peer inside, using his phone to light up the room. "Why is this open?"

"I opened it earlier." Dawson pushed past him.

"What for?" Levi remained in the doorway.

"Art supplies. Why else?" He grabbed a handful of pencils and a sketchpad.

"You broke into the art room to steal pencils and paper?" Levi asked.

Dawson pushed past him again so he could go outside, pulling the door shut behind himself. "How is that any worse than stealing chequebooks?" He returned to the table he'd sat at earlier, placing the sketchpad in front of him once he was seated. He propped his phone up so the light fell on the paper.

"What am I meant to do?" Levi stood on the other side of the table, directly in front of Dawson.

Dawson chose a pencil, shrugging rather than bothering to answer.

"What is that supposed to mean?" Levi demanded.

Dawson closed his eyes, bringing to mind the picture of the girl on the wall of the shed. Rose. Opening his eyes, he stared at Jack who stood to the side of the table. An image formed in his mind and he began to draw, lines sweeping across the page as a vague outline of two figures began to form.

He was still drawing when Burke returned, two figures now taking more shape on the page. He stood up as Burke reached the table and placed the pencil beside the sketchpad with the rest of them. He didn't know if he should ask what the verdict was or wait for Burke to tell him so he remained silent, surprised to see Burke carried the paper bag again.

"You'll need to prove yourself. I'll give you a cheque a week for the rest of this year. If they all go through with no problems, you'll get your five percent. Until then, you'll get twenty dollars a cheque."

Dawson nodded.

"Then you better get started." Burke held out the

paper bag. "Let Levi know when it's ready to be collected."

Dawson took the bag, not looking inside until the two of them strode away. He tipped the contents onto the sketchpad, momentarily closing his eyes when he realised it was another chequebook. This one contained no information on the stubs. Most of the cheques were made out for two hundred dollars. It seemed worse than Anita Gray's. He turned to Jack. "Do you know if Aiden and Lucy got the chequebook back?"

"I don't know if they've returned."

Marti came out of the shadows. "I recorded this meeting too."

"Thanks. If you want to send–" Dawson broke off at the sound of footsteps behind him. Spinning he saw Aiden and Lucy walking towards them. "Did you get the chequebook?"

Aiden shook his head, holding out his phone. "I recorded their meeting. The voices can just be heard because I recorded it from outside the window. Luckily it was open. Burke left the chequebook with Nash."

Taking the phone, Dawson watched the short clip, glancing up each time someone joined him, eventually all of them stared at the phone screen as

Burke argued out the offer, gaining ten percent per cheque starting immediately. Burke headed for the doorway, pausing in it to turn and face the man he'd earlier addressed as Nash. "I'll be back later with those other supplies you want."

"I need to go out for a couple of hours. I'll leave the back door unlocked for you."

Burke inclined his head before leaving and Nash looked at the chequebook before tossing it on a cluttered coffee table and also leaving the room. The video ended and Aiden lowered his phone.

"He's ripping you off," Xavier said. "Not that you're going through with the deal, but he doesn't know that."

"Guess there is no honour among thieves," Jack said.

"At least not these thieves." Dawson needed to explain Jack's comment when everyone looked towards him, confused. "I need to get that chequebook back. We don't know how long the police will take to sort everything out." And he wasn't about to risk a cheque, he'd forged, being used to steal Anita's money. An image of his mother came to mind, the same bright blue eyes that Morgan had. He'd so rarely seen disappointment in them when she'd looked at either him or his brother. That look had been reserved for other people. How would she have looked at him if she'd still been alive?

"Are you out of your tree?" Jack demanded.

"Are you trying to get yourself killed?" Lucy asked.

"We need to put all the videos together so we can send them to the cops," Aiden said. "The sooner they know what's going on, the sooner they can get started on bringing everyone in."

"I can put all the footage onto a USB stick and cut off any unnecessary parts at the beginning and end of each one," Jena offered.

Dawson nodded in thanks. "I'll record something to go with it." He moved to a better location, one where more light fell on him, before he began to record, making sure no one else was in the frame. "I rang, but no one seemed interested in taking me seriously. Hopefully, this is enough information that you will take it seriously now." He sent the video clip to Jena. Marti, Kobe and Aiden also sent her their footage.

"What's the address?" Dawson asked Aiden.

"I'll give you a lift," Aiden offered.

"Can you ask Jack if he can open a classroom for me so I can get started on this?" Jena held up her phone before turning to Aiden. "I'll also need the address for the police station you want me to take it to."

"I can unlock a classroom, but I think you're all making a mistake. Tell the fuzz and leave it up to them. If you can see me, then you're still in danger," Jack said.

Dawson turned to Jena. "I rang the local police station and Jack can open a classroom for you." He turned back to Jack. "And of course I'm still in danger. They haven't caught them yet, have they?"

"I'll stop in front of the classroom I need opened." Jena took a step backwards. "If he's ready to go now."

Jack sighed. "Why do none of you ever listen to me?"

Dawson grinned, glancing around the group. "That method seems to work out okay. I think I'll stick with it."

Jack slowly shook his head, a wry smile forming. "All right, but try not to get yourself killed." He glanced at Jena. "Let her know I'm ready."

Chapter Fifteen

Dawson

Dawson handed the paper bag to Jena. "This needs to be given to the cops too. And Jack is ready."

Jena took the bag. "Be careful."

Once the two of them were gone, Lucy accompanying Jena, saying none of them should be alone, Dawson turned to Aiden. "Can you give me that lift now?"

"I'll let you out up the street. We don't want to risk them seeing you arrive."

"What about us?" Kobe gestured towards himself, Xavier and Marti.

"I'll come back here after I get the chequebook."

"What if you can't get it?" Kobe asked.

Dawson didn't want to think about that option. "I'll come back here with or without it."

Marti threw her arms around Dawson. "You'll manage. I'm sure of it. Did you want us to help you?"

He awkwardly returned her hug. "I'm okay. The three of you wait here."

Marti held up the sketchpad and pencils. "I'll put these in the groundsman's shed. When you've finished it, we can hang it up next to the other pictures."

He liked that idea. It was better than someone wanting to tear it up. "Thanks." He followed Aiden to his car, getting in once it was unlocked. The drive was silent, but they didn't have far to go.

Aiden pulled up at the start of the street. "Did you want me to go with you?"

He shook his head. "Guess you better keep the getaway car ready."

Aiden chuckled. "Okay. But call me if you need any help."

"I will." Taking a deep breath, he clambered out of the car, fleetingly wondering what he was doing. An image of his mother filled his mind, the disappointed look in her eyes. The one she reserved for others. He was pretty sure she would have used it on him. Not that he didn't deserve it. He certainly did.

He headed along the side of the house. Everything was quiet. The only sounds were his footsteps. He slowed as he approached the back door. It was closed. There was just enough light spilling into the yard from some windows he was able to make his way to the back door without needing the flashlight app. He tested the handle. It was unlocked. He slipped inside, closing the door behind him.

It took him a couple of attempts to find the lounge room. The chequebook was still lying on the cluttered coffee table. He darted across the room and grabbed the chequebook, opening it to stare at the cheque he'd written out earlier. He was surprised at the amount of relief he felt. He had no idea who Anita was or what she was like. She could be completely different from his mother for all he knew. But whoever she was, she certainly didn't deserve to have her money stolen. Closing the chequebook, he shoved it in a front pocket of his jeans and headed for the back door. He reached for the handle at the same time as it opened. He froze, staring at Burke who seemed equally stunned to see him.

"Why you-" Burke broke off when Dawson spun and ran towards the front of the house.

Dawson tried not to think about how close behind him was the sound of Burke's footsteps. All he had to do was get out to Aiden's car. Reaching the front door, he tried the handle. It was locked and needed a key to open it. Spinning, he faced Burke who came to a stop in front of him in the narrow hallway.

Burke grinned. "Thought you could double cross us, did you? How did you know where I went?" He pointed to the edge of the chequebook visible in Dawson's pocket. "And I'll be having that back and you won't be getting paid for any of the cheques until the next year."

Dawson slowly reached for the chequebook, stalling for time. His gaze was drawn to the doorways leading off the hallway. Burke was between him and each of them.

Burke held out his hand. "Hurry. I haven't got all night."

Dawson lowered his head, barrelling into Burke and pushing past him, running for the closest door and slamming it shut. He turned the lock on the back of the doorknob as he scanned the room. It was filled with various items in unopened boxes. Everything from mobile phones to flat screen televisions. If he had to guess, he'd say Nash was into more than forging cheques.

Burke banged on the door. "I know where you live. And there's no point going to the cops. You're the one who forged the cheque. Not me."

Crossing the room, Dawson tried not to think of

how the door shuddered and shook. It sounded like it would burst open at any moment. He slid the curtains across, relieved to see that the window was easily opened and there were no security screens between him and escape. He climbed out the window and dropped to the ground striding around the side of the house towards the street. Behind him was a crack and he assumed Burke had busted the door open. He broke into a run, not caring about how much noise he made.

Burke pounded after him. "Perry, grab that kid."

Dawson, who'd started running towards Aiden's vehicle, went in the opposite direction when a man exited a dark sedan parked directly in front of the house. He ran down the street, hearing an engine start behind him. It sounded nothing like Aiden's car.

He angled across the street and ran down the side of a house. By the time he came out in the street behind the house's back neighbour, a dark sedan was driving towards him.

Burke leaned out the window, pointing at him. "There he is. Don't let him get away."

Dawson ran through to the next street, finding that once again they were there before him. He tried to run faster, but they gained on him. In the distance, he saw the school grounds. Not much further and he could lose himself amongst the familiar buildings. The car came alongside him and he swerved to avoid the door that was opened in front of him. He stumbled, barely remaining on his feet.

The car door was slammed shut after Burke joined him on the street, walking around behind the sedan. "You've got nowhere to go."

Dawson backed away.

"I can't help you unless you're on the school grounds," Jack said from behind Dawson.

He wanted to turn his head and see how close he was, but he didn't dare take his gaze off Burke as he continued to come closer.

"Hand over the chequebook and I won't give you the beating you deserve." Burke grinned. "I'll only rough you up a little."

"Run," Jack called out. "You're close enough now. Run."

Spinning to face Jack, Dawson broke into a run, ignoring Burke's threats. He vaulted over the fence and started towards the groundsman's shed.

Jack grabbed his arm and pulled him in a different direction. "This way. Nearly everyone else is at the groundsman's shed. You don't want to lead him there."

"Where are we going?" He kept his voice low,

aware of Burke following him through the darkened school grounds. He smiled when Burke cursed from running into something. Having Jack to lead him in the dark made a big difference.

"Eventually, back to the groundsman's shed. We need to lose Burke first."

"How are we going to do that?" Dawson glanced over his shoulder. He could hear Burke, but couldn't as yet see him.

Slowing, Jack tugged Dawson against the side of a building. "Crouch here and stay quiet. There's a shrub between you and where he'll walk."

Chapter Sixteen

Dawson

Dawson opened his mouth to ask how Jack knew where Burke would walk, but he was gone before he could speak. He crouched down as Jack had told him, listening to the approaching footsteps that slowed as they came closer, a light sweeping across the ground from Burke's phone.

The sound of a classroom door slamming open had Burke running in that direction. Another one slammed open, further away than the first one.

Dawson remained crouched beside the building, not sure if he should move. Jack had told him to wait here. Surely, it'd be okay to make his way back to the groundsman's shed while Burke was distracted. He had just about convinced himself to move when he heard footsteps coming along the side of the classroom. If he moved, whoever it was might hear him. If he remained where he was they might see him if they came around the corner. He remained still, barely daring to breathe. His phone vibrated, notifying him of an incoming message. He didn't dare move to check who it was from.

His breath escaped in a rush when he saw it was the man who'd been with Burke, the light from his phone sweeping across the ground. Perry didn't turn the corner. It was a rather ordinary name for someone who looked like they could have taken the place of the demon he'd been drawing when Levi had contacted him. It seemed so long ago now, not yesterday afternoon.

"Time to move." Jack grabbed Dawson's arm, drawing him upwards. "Before they get back here."

"What about Perry?"

"Burke called him to help check the classrooms. You've got time to get to the groundsman's shed. Aiden came back and he's given Jena a lift to the police station. When she realised I was nearby, she said to let you know that she put the USB in an envelope with your name on it and will hand it in as lost property, along with the paper bag."

He couldn't resist regularly checking over his shoulder as they made their way to the groundsman's shed even though all he could see was shadows. "How did she know you were there?"

"I interrupted the light on her phone." Jack stopped in front of the groundsman's shed. "It isn't locked."

He opened the door. "Aren't you coming in?"

"No. I need to see what they're up to. You ring the fuzz and let them know where they are."

"Okay." He'd barely stepped inside when Marti, Lucy, Kobe and Xavier all talked at once, wanting to know what was going on. Dawson held up a hand, closing the door behind him. "I need to ring the cops first."

Marti tugged the chequebook out of his pocket. "You got it back."

Dawson nodded. "Yeah, but Burke nearly caught me and is searching the school grounds for me." He called the number he'd rung earlier, holding up his hand again when Marti started to speak. "I need to report a crime."

It was just as lengthy a process as earlier, but this time he managed to talk to someone far less impatient and willing to listen to him. They did more than listen when they found the USB and the contents of the paper bag Jena had dropped off.

Jack stepped through the door. "All of you need to get out of here. They're searching the school grounds. Every single building. Levi turned up to help them."

"I have to go," Dawson said to the officer on the other end of the call. "Before Burke finds where I'm hiding."

"Where are you hiding?"

He gave the name of the school, his words greeted by silence. "I'll come into the police station."

"Good. I'd like to ask you a few questions about your school."

Jack chuckled. "I recognise that voice. You will have to be careful what you say to him."

"Okay." Dawson dreaded the thought of the upcoming interrogation.

"Let him know Perry has a gun."

Dawson passed along Jack's message.

"Are you certain?" the officer asked.

"Yeah."

"Then either hide or get somewhere safe. We'll be there shortly. Whatever you do, don't play the hero and confront him."

Dawson finished up the phone call as Aiden and Jena stepped inside. "We have to go."

Jena closed the door behind her. "Where?"

"Away from school. Burke and Perry are searching the place." Dawson stepped past her, opening the door. He froze, the door half open, Perry turning towards him. It took him only a second to start moving. He stepped outside, pulling the door closed behind him and breaking into a run.

"He's over here." Perry gave chase.

Jack came alongside him. "What do you think you're doing? You should have shut that door and stayed inside. Did you not understand the part where I said he has a gun?"

Dawson stumbled. "You going to help or lecture me?" He kept his voice low, hoping Perry couldn't hear the words.

Jack grabbed Dawson's arm, pulling him to the side. "If I don't help, you're likely to knock yourself out running into a tree." He tugged Dawson around another tree before changing the direction. "How many more times are you going to try and kill yourself?"

"I'm trying to lead him away. I don't want him to hurt any of the others."

"I don't-" Jack broke off to push Dawson from him.

Dawson collided with a tree, wrapping his arm around it to stop himself from falling. Behind him, he heard someone crash into the ground followed by Burke cursing and swearing.

Jack grabbed his arm, pulling him away from the tree. "That was close."

"Where are we going?" Dawson wished he could see more than shadows. At least having Jack to guide him meant he wasn't left stumbling around in the dark.

"Towards the school entrance. That seems to be where the fuzz turn up."

Dawson's legs ached from all the running he'd been doing. He wasn't completely inactive, but he did spend more time drawing than doing anything else. "Are you sure that's a good idea? There's more light towards the front entrance." He'd put some distance between Burke and Perry, their footsteps not sounding as close.

"I will kill you," Burke called out. "Do you hear me, Dawson? I will kill you."

"Ignore him. Keep running," Jack ordered.

"I'm not an idiot." Dawson glanced over his shoulder, but could see nothing, other than shadows.

"You're out of your tree with some of the stuff you've done tonight," Jack said.

"What does that mean?" Dawson asked. "Being out of your tree. What exactly does it mean?"

"Mad. Crazy. Insane."

Dawson had thought it meant he was an idiot.

He laughed softly. "I can't argue that." He stumbled when Jack pulled him to the right. "What are you trying to do? Help them catch me?"

Jack started to speak, breaking off to push Dawson to the ground.

Dawson collided with the ground as a gunshot rang out. He rolled over onto his back as Burke bellowed his name. He started to rise.

Jack pushed him back down. "Don't move. He didn't see exactly where you landed. He's searching the wrong spot."

Burke now used his phone to search the area. "You will regret you ever crossed me."

Dawson was beginning to regret he'd ever forged the permission slip for Levi. He would have been better off letting himself get caught. The two of them would have been in trouble because he would have mentioned that Levi had tried to blackmail him. He thought of the cheque. One Burke would never get to cash in. Anita Gray's cheque.

"Something moved." Perry fired his gun.

"Don't move from there," Jack said. "They won't be able to see you as long as you stay still."

"Are you trying to kill him?" Burke demanded.

"You were the one threatening to kill him," Perry pointed out.

Dawson wanted to ask Jack why they wouldn't be able to see him. Except with how close the two of them sounded, even with the light from Burke's phone pointed in the other direction, they'd definitely find him if he spoke.

"Threatening isn't actually-" Burke broke off as the area was flooded with light.

"Drop your weapons. This is the police."

Perry and Burke broke into a run, the police giving chase.

There was now enough light that Dawson could see a low shrub kept him hidden. He looked to the side where he'd last heard Jack. He was no longer there. "Jack? Are you there?" He kept his voice low even though the sounds of pursuit faded into the distance.

His question was greeted by silence. No one spoke and no one moved.

He half sat up. "Jack?" His voice was slightly louder.

"Dawson! Are you still here, Dawson?"

He lay back against the ground, recognising the voice of the officer he'd talked to on the phone.

"Dawson! It's safe to come out. We have your two pursuers in custody."

Dawson remained where he was until the sound

of the officer calling out to him grew faint. Sitting up, he tried to see what was in the area. Once again everything was in shadows. He slowly made his way towards the groundsman's shed. He needed to let everyone else know Burke had been caught. After that, he'd talk to the police.

Reaching the groundsman's shed, it struck him. Like the others, he'd never get to speak to Jack again. He'd lost his chance to thank him for everything he'd done. He understood now why everyone had wanted him to give a message to Jack for them.

Chapter Seventeen

Jack

Jack stood beside Dawson, wondering what he was doing standing in front of the groundsman's shed staring at it. Not that Dawson would be able to clearly see it in the dark. "Blasted bird," he muttered.

Dawson stepped forward and knocked softly on the door of the groundsman's shed. "Is everyone still in there?"

Marti partially opened the door. Grabbing hold of Dawson's hand, she dragged him inside. "I didn't know who was knocking." She closed the door.

Jack stepped through the closed door, not locking it on them. They would need to get out eventually.

"What happened?" Xavier asked.

"The cops caught Burke. Caught both of them." Dawson glanced towards the door. "I need to go talk to them, but I wanted to let all of you know it was safe to come out." He grinned. "Although you may not want to leave by the main entrance while the cops are here. They'll probably have questions."

Marti laughed. "Trust me. They'll have hundreds of questions. Especially about why you came here."

Jack chuckled, remembering all of Marti's complaints about the many questions the fuzz had asked her.

"I'm not going out there," Xavier said. "I've spent enough time this year being grounded."

Kobe grinned. "Yeah, if you don't need us to talk to the police, I wouldn't mind avoiding getting into trouble."

Dawson looked at each of them. "You know, we could do this again. Help people like Jack helped us. They don't have to be life threatening situations."

Marti slowly nodded. "That's a great idea."

Jena nodded too. "Kids who are being bullied, or having problems at home."

"Yes," Lucy said. "We can help all those who have no one to turn to. Like Jack had no one to turn to."

"How do we find them?" Xavier asked.

"By being observant," Aiden said.

"And by listening," Lucy added.

Jack stared at them as they made plans, bursting

with the need to talk to someone. To share the moment with someone who'd be as excited as he was. He'd never once expected anything like this. He followed them as they went outside, still making plans, talking and laughing together, Dawson saying several times that he really should talk to the police.

The angel appeared beside Jack, nodding towards the group who stood out the front of the groundsman's shed. "This will have long reaching effects. You've surprised me, Jack. And surprised others."

Jack had no idea what to say, so he remained silent. It was probably better than getting into an argument with the blasted bird and ruining the moment.

"Nothing to say for yourself?"

Jack shrugged. Probably nothing he wanted to hear. The only comment he wanted to make was to demand why he couldn't have a few minutes with them so he could say goodbye.

"You finally did it."

Jack frowned. "Did what?" He really wished the blasted bird could try and make an effort to be more easily understood.

"Atoned for your sins."

He faced the angel. "Atoned..." His voice trailed off. Surely not. He hadn't done nearly enough. Not to atone for taking two lives as well as the other many small offences.

"It's time for you to go on. To leave this place. Your mother has been waiting for you," the angel said.

Jack glanced in the direction of those he'd helped. They'd now reached the fence and had paused there to talk, the words indistinct from this distance. "What about the students? Who will help them?"

"You've done your part. They will manage on their own." The angel smiled, one that had no hint of mockery in it for a change. "You can't save everyone, Jack."

The smile bothered Jack. It took him a few seconds to figure out why. There was a touch of sorrow in it. "Do I have a choice?"

The angel's smile faded. "A choice about what in particular?"

"If I leave or stay."

"You wish to stay."

Jack almost laughed at the disbelief he could hear in the angel's tone. "Not just stay, but stay and help the students that find themselves in trouble. Is that possible?"

The angel examined him. "You have changed in the past year. The time you've spent helping the students has done you more good than the years you were meant to spend contemplating your sins."

"I've never been much for over thinking the situation," Jack said.

"That is an understatement," the angel said dryly.

This time Jack did grin. "I suppose so." He paused a moment. "Can I stay?" This was his school. They were his students. He wasn't about to desert them if it was possible to stay.

The angel inclined his head. "You can stay, but think very carefully before you decide. The offer to move on might not come again for a very long time. If at all."

He thought of his mother, leaning over him as his life ebbed away. As much as he'd like to see her and apologise for what he'd done, the students needed him. How many would have died if he hadn't been here? "Will everything be the same? Will you still tell me who needs help and will they still be able to see and hear me while I help them?"

"A few things will change. You won't need me to tell you who needs help. You'll know who's in danger. And when you decide to help them, they will be able to interact with you. One other thing will change."

He dreaded to know what that one thing would

be, especially since the blasted bird didn't say. It was probably bad. Something he'd find impossible to put up with. But he had to know. It wouldn't make a difference. No matter what it was, he wouldn't desert them. "What will change?"

"That is up to you."

Frowning, Jack played the angel's words over in his mind. They made no sense. "I don't get what you mean."

"You can make one change. What will it be? The ability to leave the school grounds? You've complained about that often enough. A limited ability of being able to interact with the world around you? Something else?"

"One change." He could hardly believe he was being offered something good rather than having something bad dumped on him. He'd been certain he wasn't going to like what the angel had to say.

"Only one and it can't be life. It doesn't work that way," the angel said.

He thought fleetingly of being able to leave the school grounds or of being able to interact with the world around him, even if it was only in a limited way. He would have liked either of those, but there was one thing he had to ask for. It was for the students as much as it was for him. "I want to be able to see and talk to all those I've helped even after I've helped them." He frowned when the angel studied him again, worried the blasted bird would say no. "Or at least have a warning that they're out of danger so they can have a few minutes to say goodbye."

"Once again you have surprised me, Jack. I would have expected you to ask for something for yourself." The angel rested his hand on Jack's shoulder. "This is your task now. This school is yours to watch over and all those you help will forever be able to interact with you as if you were living. You will not need the moment of you fading from their lives to know they're no longer in danger. That ability comes with the one that lets you know who is in danger." The angel lowered his hand, stepping back.

He felt no different. "That's it? I'll be able to talk to them and they'll be able to hear me?" He glanced towards the fence where the seven of them remained, talking animatedly.

"What did you expect? Trumpets and angels singing?" the angel asked dryly.

Jack laughed at the familiar tone. "No, but…" His voice trailed off. "Thank you."

The angel inclined his head before vanishing.

Jack stared at the spot for a moment before looking towards the fence. They were still there. All those he'd helped. Kobe placed his hands on the fence like he was about to vault over it. He couldn't let them leave. Not without telling them they could now hear him. Kobe vaulted over the fence, the rest of them doing the same.

Jack broke into a run. He reached the fence as they reached the other side of the road, still talking. He was too late. It was impossible for him to leave the school grounds. Their laughter reached him. A smile formed. Surely they weren't too far away. "Marti!"

Marti stopped, turning to face him, her mouth hanging open for a moment before she laughed and ran back towards him, her companions doing the same. She stood on the other side of the fence. "I can see you."

He nodded, momentarily lost for words at her expression. He had never seen her so happy before.

"Jack! I can see you." Marti vaulted over the fence, throwing her arms around him. "Say something, Jack. Tell me I'm not imagining things.

Jack laughed. "You're not imagining things." He returned her hug before letting her go.

Kobe chuckled, vaulting over the fence. "If you're imagining things, then I am too." He clapped Jack on the shoulder. "It's good to see you again."

Dawson vaulted the fence along with the rest of

them. "I wanted to thank you." He held out his hand. "For everything you did."

Jack shook his hand. "No. I'm the one who should thank you." Letting go of Dawson's hand, he looked at each of them. "I need to thank all of you."

Dawson frowned. "Why? We didn't do anything."

Jack nodded. "Because of each of you and your plans for the future, I've atoned for my sins."

"This is it?" Marti asked. "This is goodbye?" She clung to his arm. "They're letting you say goodbye?"

Jack shook his head. "No. This is only the beginning." He grinned. "And I have all of you to thank for it. This is my school. I'm here to stay for good."

Laughing, Marti threw her arms around him, the rest crowding in to do the same. "I can't wait to see what the next year brings. It will be amazing."

Jack laughed. He certainly hoped so.

Free Ebook

Subscribe to Avril's newsletter and receive a free ebook. This ebook is exclusive to those on her mailing list. To find out more about this offer visit:

www.avrilsabine.com/free-ebook

*

We value your privacy and will not sell, rent, exchange or loan your email address to third parties. Your information is confidential and you are under no obligation to remain on the mailing list and can unsubscribe at any time.

Acknowledgements

As I wrap up this series, I can't help thinking back over all those who've helped me with it along the way. Thank you. To all of you. I appreciate the help you've given me.

To The Reader

If you enjoyed this book, why not consider leaving a review to help other readers discover it too? Reader engagement is one of the few ways that lets an author know readers want more books in a particular series or genre. So leave a review and tell friends, not only about this book but also about other ones you've enjoyed, so you can continue to enjoy books by your favourite authors for years to come.

Dreams are meant to be lived,

Avril.

About The Author

Avril is an Australian author who lives with her family on acreage in South East Queensland. She writes mostly young adult and children's speculative fiction, but has been known to dabble in other genres. You can find more information about her at www.avrilsabine.com where you can also subscribe to her newsletter to be kept informed about new releases, current projects, blog posts and exclusive news.

Titles By Avril Sabine

Stories about strong characters and characters who discover their strengths.

SERIES

Assassins Of The Dead- Young Adult Fantasy/ Paranormal

Book 1: Dark Blade

Book 2: Dragon Touched

Book 3: Society Against Vampires

Book 4: King's Request

Dragon Blood- Young Adult Urban Fantasy (with elements of romance)

(5 book series)

Book 1: Pliethin

Book 2: Wyvern

Book 3: Surety

Book 4: Knight

Book 5: Mage

Dragon Mage- Young Adult Urban Fantasy (with elements of romance)

(Series two of Dragon Blood series)

Book 1: Promise

Dragon Blood Chronicles- Young Adult Urban Fantasy (with elements of romance)

(Companion stand alone series to Dragon Blood)

Book 1: Oath

Book 2: Betrayed

Guardians Of The Round Table- Young Adult Fantasy LitRPG

(Co-written with Storm and Rhys Petersen)

Book 1: Dexterity Fail

Book 2: Goblin Boots

Book 3: Singed Feathers

Book 4: Frog Mage

Book 5: Crystal Mine

Book 6: Cursed Harp

Rosie's Rangers- Young Adult Western Steampunk

(6 book series)

Book 1: Justice

Book 2: Vengeance

Book 3: Treachery

Book 4: Accused

Book 5: Wanted

Book 6: Corruption

Mark Of Kings- Children's Fantasy

(Upper middle grade/preteen)

(4 book series)

Book 1: The Arena

Book 2: The Island

Book 3: The Assassin

Book 4: The King

STAND ALONE SERIES

Demon Hunters- Young Adult Urban Fantasy/ Horror (with elements of romance)

Book 1: Blood Sacrifice

Book 2: Retribution

Book 3: Tainted

Book 4: Premonition

Book 5: Cursed

Book 6: Feud

Book 7: Extrication

Plea Of The Damned- Young Adult Urban Fantasy/Paranormal

(6 book series)

Book 1: Forgive Me Lucy

Book 2: Forgive Me Aiden

Book 3: Forgive Me Jena

Book 4: Forgive Me Kobe

Book 5: Forgive Me Marti

Book 6: Forgive Me Dawson

Realms Of The Fae- Young Adult Urban Fantasy (with elements of romance)

The Sword (short story in Like A Girl Anthology)

Heart Of Stone

Book 1: A Debt Owed

Book 2: Marked By The Hunt

Book 3: The Magic Collector

Book 4: An Unexpected Betrayal

Book 5: Imprisoned By Iron

Fairytales Retold (Short Stories)

Snow-White And Rose-Red

The Twelve Brothers

The Light Princess

Beauty And The Beast

Sleeping Beauty

Aschenputtel

The Golden Bird

The Frog Prince

The Death Of Koshchei The Deathless

Myths And Legends Retold (Short Stories)

Ion, Son Of Apollo

Sir Gawain And The Maid With The Narrow Sleeves

Princess Ilse, The Giant's Daughter

YOUNG ADULT NOVELS

Young Adult Fantasy (with elements of romance)

Elf Sight

Earth Bound

Young Adult Urban Fantasy

Stone Warrior (with elements of romance)

The Jungle Inside

Young Adult Contemporary (with elements of romance)

Through Your Eyes

The Ugly Stepsister

Perfect Little Princess

Young Adult Contemporary/Paranormal

Whispers In The Dark (with elements of romance and same sex relationships)

Over Too Soon (with elements of romance)

Young Adult Sci-Fi

Experiment X-One-Six (Urban Sci-Fi/Superheroes)

An Endless Dawn (Post Apocalyptic Sci-Fi)

CHILDREN'S BOOKS

Dragon Lord (Preteen/early teens) (Fantasy)

The Irish Wizard (Upper middle grade) (Urban Fantasy)

SHORT STORIES

Urban Fantasy

Eternally Late

Dealings With Joe

Glimpses (short story in That Moment When Anthology)

Contemporary

The Brat Next Door

Fantasy LitRPG

(Set in the same world as Guardians Of The Round Table Series)

Tales Of Inadon 1: The Disc (Co-written with Storm and Rhys Petersen) (short story in Game On! Anthology)

Post Apocalyptic Sci-Fi

Compulsive Directive

NONFICTION

A Year Of Weekly Writing Exercises (Creative Writing)

Cooking For Families With Allergies (Cooking) (Co-written with Storm Petersen)

Tell Me A Story, Grandma (Memoir)

For the most up to date details on available titles visit:

www.avrilsabine.com/books/bibliography

Plea Of The Damned Series

To learn more about this series visit:

www.avrilsabine.com/series/potd

BOOKS AVAILABLE IN THE PLEA OF THE DAMNED SERIES:

Book 1: Forgive Me Lucy

Book 2: Forgive Me Aiden

Book 3: Forgive Me Jena

Book 4: Forgive Me Kobe

Book 5: Forgive Me Marti

Book 6: Forgive Me Dawson

Disclaimer

This is a work of fiction. Names, characters, businesses, places, events and incidents are either the products of the author's imagination or used in a fictitious manner. Any resemblance to actual persons, living or dead, or actual events is purely coincidental. The opinions expressed or beliefs held are those of the characters and should not be assumed to be the opinions or beliefs of the author.

www.ingramcontent.com/pod-product-compliance
Lightning Source LLC
Chambersburg PA
CBHW031418200726
48285CB00017BA/2443